CONTENTS

Young Mike Evans travels the world with his dino-hunting dad. From the Jurassic Coast in Dorset to the Liaoning Province in China, young Dino-Mike has been there, *dug* that!

While his dad is dusting fossils, Mike's busy refining his own dino skills – only he's out discovering the real thing. A live T. rex egg! A portal to the Jurassic Period!! An undersea dinosaur sanctuary!!!

Prepare yourself for another wild and wacky Dino-Mike adventure, one which nobody will ever believe...

Chapter 1

ROAR!

Inside a small tent, Mike Evans lay in his sleeping bag. A lamp flickered next to him. Outside, frogs croaked in the cool spring night.

Suddenly, a large shadow appeared on the wall of the tent. A T. rex!

"ROOOAAR!!" growled a voice.

"Ahh!" screamed Mike, jumping up.

"Haha!" laughed Mike's dad, Stanley.
He was twisting his hands in front of
the lamp's light. "Not bad for a shadow
puppet, hey, Mike?"

"Very funny, Dad," said Mike, settling
back into his sleeping bag. "Now I'll
never sleep."

"You should try to sleep," his dad said. "You never know, perhaps tomorrow we'll dig up a *real* tyrannosaurus rex."

"Do you think?" Mike asked excitedly.

"If we're lucky," his dad replied. He turned off the lamp. "Did you know the first T. rex fossils were found –?"

"Here in Montana, USA in 1902," Mike interrupted.

"Wow!" his dad exclaimed. "You know your dino facts! But did you know the T. rex is a theropod, meaning –?"

"It walked on two legs instead of four." Mike laughed. "You asked me that question last week, remember, Dad?"

"Oh yes!, Oh, and I nearly forgot..." said his dad. He reached into his rucksack and pulled out a present. "As this is your first archaeological dig, I've got you a present."

"Thanks, Dad!" Mike ripped open the present like a hungry dinosaur.

He pulled a shiny green jacket out of the box. "Clothes?" he asked, obviously disappointed.

"This is *special* jacket, Mike. A scientist friend of mine developed it," explained his dad. He ran his fingers over the fabric. "These scales look and act like the scales of a real dinosaur."

Mike gasped. "Wow! Really?"

"Yes," his dad replied. "Try it on."

Mike scrambled out of his sleeping bag and put on the jacket. "It's perfect!" he exclaimed.

"That's not all," said his dad. He reached over Mike's shoulder and pulled the hood onto his head. "It's a hoodie!"

Mike's dad held up a mirror. The hood looked just like the head of a T. rex! A row of razor-sharp teeth lined the fringe. Two large yellow eyes glowed on either side of the hood.

Mike's dad clicked a button on the jacket's sleeve. **Beep! Beep!** The T. rex eyes lit up like headlights.

"Wow!" shouted Mike.

His dad clicked another button. **Pop! Pop! Pop!** Three diamond shapes burst from the back of the jacket.

"Are those –" Mike began.

"Yes," his dad answered before his son could finish. "Stegosaurus plates! Actually, they're solar panels to power the jacket. They'll also keep the jacket nice and warm."

Mike hugged his dad. "This is the best present ever!"

"I'm glad you like it, Mike," said his dad, "and I'm glad you're here with me." He slipped back into his sleeping bag. "Now let's get some sleep. We have a whole day of dinosaur digging ahead of us tomorrow."

"Okay, Dad," Mike replied.

Mike lay down, pulled his sleeping
bag up to his neck, and let his head sink
into the pillow. He smiled.

Mike couldn't wait for
the adventure to begin!

Chapter 2

T. REX!

"It's a T. rex!" shouted Mike's dad.

Other palaeontologists ran over. The scientists carried shovels, pick axes and brushes. They all stared at a giant bone sticking out of the ground.

"Good find, Dad," said Mike. Wearing his new Dino Jacket, he squeezed in between the scientists for a closer look.

Mike zipped up his jacket and shook off the morning chill. The sun had barely risen, and the team had already been digging for hours.

"Does finding fossils always take this long?" Mike asked his dad.

"It certainly does," his dad replied. He used a small brush to remove tiny bits of dirt from the T. rex bone. "We don't want the fossils to break!"

Mike kicked a few rocks on the ground and sighed.

"Say," added his dad, "why don't you go and explore some of the other dig sites."

"Can I?" asked Mike excitedly.

"Of course," replied his dad, "but be back before it gets dark, okay? We're going to the big Dinosaur BBQ tonight."

"I wouldn't miss it!" said Mike, licking his lips. Then he looked around to see which direction he should go in.

Mike explored several dig sites. There were scientists at every site, digging or sifting through small fragments of bone.

"Borrring!" Mike said, yawning.

Just then, a flash of colour caught the corner of his eye. A red-haired girl stood at the edge of a nearby forest. He watched as she slipped into the trees and away from the dig site.

Where's she going? wondered Mike. He ran towards a tall tree and started to climb it to gain a better view.

Fwip! Fwip! Two sets of shiny white hooks burst from the cuffs of his Dino Jacket. They dug into the tree bark.

"Velociraptor claws!" Mike exclaimed.

With help from the claws, Mike quickly reached the top of the tree. He looked out over the forest but couldn't see the mysterious girl.

Then something caught Mike's eye. On the forest floor, he spotted what looked like a large, slimy lizard tail. It slithered quickly out of sight.

"A dinosaur tail!!" shouted Mike.

He scrambled out of the tree and started running back to the dig site. A moment later, he realized that what he had seen couldn't possibly be a dinosaur.

Suddenly a figure appeared in front of him. "Ahhh!" Mike screamed, sliding to a stop on the muddy forest floor.

Mike looked up. Standing in front of him was the mysterious redhead.

"Why are you following me?" the girl asked, pointing a finger at him.

"I w-wasn't really," Mike stammered as he stood up. "I was just w-wondering where you were going."

"Not that it's any of your business," the girl said, "but I was tracking something."

"A *dinosaur*?" Mike joked.

"Did you see it?" the girl shouted. "Where did it go?" She pulled out a small, hi-tech gadget. It was about the size of a mobile phone. Mike couldn't see what the screen was displaying.

BOOOM! BOOOOM!

"Did you hear that?" she asked Mike.

"No, I didn't hear anything –"

BOOOM! BOOOOM!

The girl cut Mike off before he could finish his sentence. "There it is again!" The girl looked down at the ground and shuddered. "Uh-oh."

Mike followed her eyes to the ground to see what she was looking at. He wondered why she was staring at a muddy puddle until he noticed ripples on the surface of the water. The ripples grew bigger and bigger. Something was getting closer and closer.

"We need to run," said the girl as she began to back away from the puddle.

"Why?" asked Mike.

Answering his question, a giant T. rex charged out of the forest towards them.

ROOOAAR!

Chapter 3
RUN!

"Keep running!" the girl shouted.

Mike tried keeping up with her. He could feel the steamy breath of the real-life tyrannosaurus rex chasing them.

Between gasps for air, Mike managed to ask, "How ... is this ... possible?"

"It's a long story," the girl replied, ducking under a tree branch. "But, yes, he's the real thing!"

27

Mike glanced behind him. "That can't possibly be a *real* dinosaur!" he said, trying to convince himself.

The girl suddenly turned left. Mike followed. The T. rex tracked the redhead as though she had a target on her back.

"Your hair!" Mike exclaimed.

"What about it?" replied the girl between breaths.

"The T. rex," explained Mike, "he's following the colour of your hair!"

"Oh my gosh!" said the girl. "My hood. I forgot!"

The girl quickly pulled her jacket hood over her bright red hair and then jumped behind a tree. Mike did the same.

Beneath the cover of the leaves, the duo kept as quiet as possible.

BOOOM! BOOOOM! The giant lizard stomped past them. His footsteps soon faded into the distance.

"Are you okay? Good," said the girl, not waiting for Mike's reply. "The best thing you can do is get out of here before that beast comes back."

The girl got up and looked around. Then she walked off in the direction the T. rex had just taken.

"Wait!" Mike called after her. "Where are you going?"

"I have work to do," she replied.

"B-but," Mike stuttered, "w-what w-was that thing?"

The girl continued walking away. "If you don't know what a dinosaur is," she said, "I don't have time to explain."

"I know what a dinosaur is. That was a tyrant lizard king!" Mike shouted. He used the meaning of the T. rex's scientific name to prove how much he knew about dinosaurs. "But they became extinct more than 65 million years ago!"

"I'm not surprised that you know so much," said the girl. "You're Mike Evans, aren't you?"

"How do you know that?" he asked.

"Your father is one of the leading palaeontologists in the country," she replied. "I was thinking about asking him for some help, but he's – how do I put this nicely – an adult."

The girl stopped. "You seem to know a lot about dinosaurs," she said. "How much do you *really* know?"

"Ask me anything," he said.

"Okay." The girl smirked. "What's the spiky tail of a stegosaurus called?"

"A thagomizer," Mike quickly replied. "Now answer *me* a question. Let's pretend all of this is true. Let's pretend it's a real dinosaur, and you're going out there to look for it. What will you do when you find it?"

"Ha! That's a silly question, Mike," she said. "I'm going to blast that dino back to the past, of course!"

Chapter 4

MYSTERY GIRL

Mike followed the girl back to her campsite. When they arrived, he stepped inside the girl's small tent.

"'Wow!" he exclaimed. The inside of the tent was filled with hi-tech gadgets and equipment. Piles of lights, buttons and switches glowed all around.

"Who are you?" asked Mike, puzzled.

"I'm lots of things," said the girl. "But today, I'm a T. rex tracker."

"Tyrannosaurs are extinct!" Mike insisted. "They don't exist anymore."

"You still don't believe that what you saw was real?" asked the girl. "You saw it with your own eyes. What else could it have been?"

"A Yeti?" suggested Mike.

"Please tell me you're joking," the girl said.

"Well, whatever that creature is," he began, ignoring her question, "how are you going to send it back to the past?"

The girl held an impressive-looking gadget that Mike didn't recognize. "We are going to *track* him with this!"

The girl held up a different gadget with her other hand. "And then we'll *catch* him with this," she explained.

Mike stared blankly at her.

"Come on," she said. "When will you have another chance to catch a T. rex?"

Mike couldn't help but smile at the thought. "That would be amazing," he told the mysterious girl.

"Good," she said, walking towards the tent's opening. "Now, come on, let's go and get that dino!"

"Wait," Mike called after her. "I don't even know your name."

The girl shuffled and fumbled with the equipment in her arms in order to free her hand. She held it out towards Mike. "My name is Shannon," she said.

"Nice to meet you, Shannon," Mike replied, shaking her hand firmly.

Chapter 5

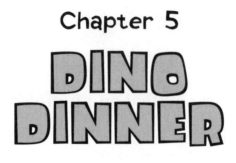

DINO DINNER

Shannon turned on the hi-tech scanner. "This little machine reports the location of any nearby creature larger than an elephant," she said. "You don't get elephants in Montana, do you?"

"No," replied Mike.

Shannon pointed to a red dot on the scanner's screen. "Then *that's* our dino!"

"Really?!" Mike exclaimed.

"Yes," answered Shannon, "and he's heading towards the main dig site. I think he must be looking for food."

Mike turned to run. "We have to stop that T. rex," he shouted, "before it eats anyone!"

Shannon ran to keep up with Mike. "T. rex are more likely to scavenge than hunt, you know?" she explained.

"I know that," Mike replied. "But I can't take the risk of my dad becoming dino dinner!"

"How do you plan to stop him?" asked Shannon.

Mike stopped. "You said yourself that tyrannosaurs are scavengers, but how do they find their food?"

Shannon thought for a second. "Their olfactory senses are actually quite tremendous."

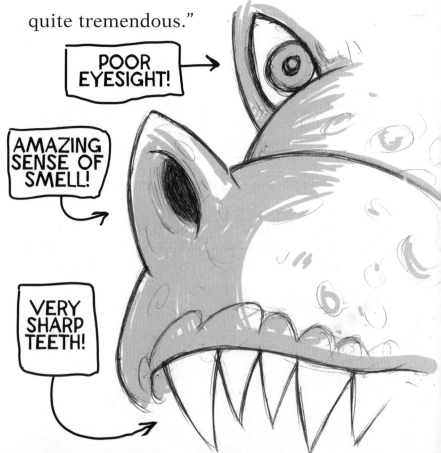

"Exactly!" Mike exclaimed. "The T. rex has a *monster* sense of smell."

Mike turned and started running off in a different direction.

"Where are you going?" asked Shannon. "The dig site is this way."

"Yes," said Mike, "but base camp is over there."

Shannon didn't understand, but she followed anyway. When they reached base camp, they hid behind a group of trees. The area was filled with picnic tables, rows of barbecues, and everything else you could ever possibly need for outdoor cooking.

A few people were hanging a giant banner that read *DINOSAUR BBQ*.

"Why are we here?" Shannon asked.

Mike pointed. "For that!"

"Hot dogs?" Shannon wondered aloud. "Have we come all this way because you're hungry?"

Mike smiled at her and said, "No, but I think that the T. rex is starving..."

Chapter 6

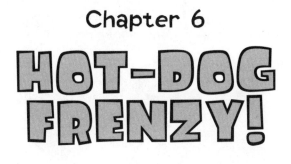

"Are you sure you know how to drive this thing?" Mike asked Shannon.

The hot-dog van sped down the hillside at top speed.

"Not really," replied Shannon to Mike's terrified reaction to her driving. "It can't be that difficult. After all, it has a giant picture of a hot dog on it!"

A thought flashed into Mike's mind. The last time he was at an amusement park, Mike's dad insisted he kept his arms and legs inside the ride. He was grateful for that advice now as Shannon narrowly missed a tree.

"Why don't you let me drive?" Mike asked Shannon.

Shannon glanced at him and joked, "You don't look old enough to drive."

Although technically true, Mike didn't think he had time to explain that he'd spent most of the summer holidays go-carting with his friends.

"Well, at least slow down a bit!" said Mike, raising his voice.

He held on as they took another sharp turn to avoid an oak tree. The van jumped over some rocks, nearly throwing Mike out over the window. The lid on the top of the hot-dog trailer flew open. Mike could see the hot dogs bouncing around inside. Some started jumping out.

Mike climbed out of his seat to close the lid. He needed every single hot dog for his plan (which might not even work!).

Just as he began to crawl back, his hand felt strange, as if there was a sudden shift in temperature. Warmer and more humid – wait! Someone was breathing on his hand. Mike's eyes moved from his hand upwards. Not someone. SomeTHING. Something enormous was breathing on his hand!

"Quick," Mike muttered. "Faster!"

Shannon huffed. "Make your mind up! Do you want me to slow down or go faster?"

Mike moved to the front of the trailer, crawling as far away from the T. rex as possible. "Definitely go faster!"

"ROOOAAR!"

Shannon didn't need to turn around to know what was behind them.

If the piercing roar wasn't enough of a clue, the blast of hot air from the dinosaur's breath that certainly was.

"We're almost at the dig site!" Mike shouted. "There's only one way to see if Mr Dino's olfactory system is working – make sure he gets a good sniff of those hot dogs."

"Yes! Do it!" shouted Shannon as the T. rex loomed closer.

Mike picked up a handful of hot dogs and threw them out of the back of the trailer. There was a loud **SNAP** as the giant T. rex jaws grabbed the hot dogs out of the air.

"We've got his attention. Now let's see if we can keep it!" said Shannon. She steered the van away from the dig sites.

Mike threw some more hot dogs into the air.

"It's working!" he exclaimed as the dinosaur turned to follow them. "Although I'm not sure why I'm so excited that we have just encouraged a huge T. rex to follow us!"

"You're excited because you're about to catch your first dino," said Shannon.

Mike didn't know whether to agree with her about that.

"Get ready to jump!" Shannon shouted.

"Why...?!" Mike exclaimed. But the only response he got was the sight of Shannon leaping out of the van.

Needing no further instruction, Mike jumped off to the side just in time to see the T. rex jaws clamp down on the back of the hot dog trailer. **CRUNCH!**

Mike hit the ground hard and rolled to a stop. Behind him, he watched the dino rip apart the trailer like an eggshell. Within seconds, the beast had eaten nearly every single hot dog.

"Shannon!" Mike said, scrambling to his feet.

Shannon was already busy preparing her equipment. Mike hesitated at first, not wanting to interrupt her, but then asked, "What do we do now?"

Without looking up, she replied, "Now that we've got him right where we want him..."

"This is where we want him?" Mike asked. "In the middle of the forest eating hot dogs?" He gestured towards the dinosaur. "Which, by the way, he's almost finished, and I think he might still be hungry."

"Exactly. Hopefully he'll come after us next." Shannon smiled.

Mike began to agree with her. "Yes, hopefully ... wait, come after US?!"

Just then, the T. rex gobbled up the last of the hot dogs and turned towards them.

"Um, I think we better run ... again," said Mike, pulling on the elbow of Shannon's sleeve.

Instead, Shannon moved forward towards the oncoming T. rex. She flipped open one of her gadgets and slid it across the ground towards the giant lizard.

Fwoosh! A blue laser-light beam burst from the gadget and formed a cube even bigger than the dinosaur.

Mike was confused. The blue cube was empty. He could see the outline that made up the edges of the cube, but it looked like nothing more than a hologram. It was certainly not enough to hold a T. rex back for long.

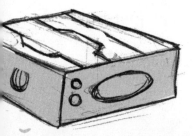

"Shannon, I don't think this is a good idea," Mike said.

Mike closed his eyes so he didn't have to look at what he thought was about to happen. A split second later, he opened one eye to take a peek.

The T. rex entered the blue cube, and to Mike's surprise the beast suddenly froze. Everything went quiet. The pounding footsteps no longer thundered. The heavy breathing of the massive creature stopped. The forest became peaceful once again.

Now Mike opened both eyes. He looked up to see that the T. rex was hypnotized. Mike marvelled at just how big, strong and dangerous it appeared.

"Wow." It was the only thing Mike could think to say. "How did you do that?"

"We call it a Trap-o-saur," Shannon said. "The safest way to catch dinos."

"He's ... he's not in any pain, is he?" Mike asked, worried.

"No," Shannon explained. "I would never hurt a living creature. The trap puts the dinosaurs that enter its field into a sort of suspended animation. It's a bit like they're asleep but actually they're awake."

"Is it permanent?" asked Mike.

"No," she said. "He'll stay this way until we can come back and pick him up." She started gathering her other equipment. "Once we get him back where he belongs, he'll be released from the trap and he'll be absolutely fine."

"Now that the danger is over," said Mike, "I'm going to miss having a dinosaur running around the place. Except for him wanting to eat us, of course!"

Shannon and Mike started to walk away from the dinosaur. "Mike," Shannon began, "you've been a big help. I don't know how to say thank you."

Mike chuckled. "Any time you need someone to help you chase a dinosaur," he said, "call me."

Then, a **CRUNCH** echoed through the forest behind them. Shannon and Mike both froze in their tracks.

"Did you just hear that?" asked Mike.

Mike turned around slowly.

"It sounded like…" Shannon began.

CRUNCH came the sound again from behind them.

"The footsteps of a dinosaur!" Mike finished her thought.

Mike and Shannon looked at each other, not wanting to turn around. When they did, the duo spotted their old friend: T. rex! The oversized beast had broken free from his trap.

CRUNCH! CRASH! He stomped towards them, even angrier than before.

"H-how did he break free?" said Mike.

"I don't know," answered Shannon. "The only way he could get out of the Trap-o-saur would be if –"

"Someone let him out?" came a nearby voice.

A shadowy figure stepped out from behind a tree.

The stranger was holding a something. It looked like the same type of gadget that Shannon had used. The gadget had a red laser-like blade, which had obviously just been used to cut through the blue laser cube that had been holding the T. rex.

"Let me guess," said Shannon, "*you* set the T. rex free?"

Mike was surprised by this stranger but noticed that Shannon was not.

"I thought you might still be here," Shannon added.

"Of course," said the stranger. "I had to make sure the T. rex I brought here got the chance to stay here."

As the T. rex stepped closer to Shannon and Mike, the mysterious figure stepped out of the shadows. He was a tall boy, older than Mike and Shannon by a year or two.

He was wearing a purple shirt and black trousers. Mike could barely see the stranger's eyes as his hair almost covered them completely.

Mike was about to ask the person who he was when he heard Shannon mutter a name...

"Jurassic Jeff."

Chapter 7

JURASSIC JEFF

"Who?" asked Mike.

"Jeff," answered the stranger. "That's me. I'm the one and only Jurassic Jeff."

Mike said, "Your parents actually called you Jurassic Jeff?"

CRUNCH! SMASH! CRUNCH!

Just then, the T. rex advanced slowly towards Mike and Shannon.

The stranger smiled. "I think you've got more important things to worry about than my name," he said, "like a giant T. rex coming straight for you!"

"Jeff," Shannon pleaded.

The T. rex stomped a clawed foot towards them. **Whump!** Shannon started to back away. "I know I've said this before but ... RUN!" she screamed.

"You don't need to say that twice," Mike responded, following closely behind her.

The T. rex gave chase. They could hear Jurassic Jeff call out, "See you around Shannon ... *maybe*."

The duo ran under fallen logs, between overgrown plants and over rocks. The T. rex easily crossed, crushed and smashed through each obstacle.

"He's not stopping!" huffed Mike.

The duo finally stopped in an area surrounded by tall trees. With the T. rex behind them, they turned and backed up until they were against a large boulder. They were both too tired to go on.

Nearly out of breath, Shannon said, "I can't … run … anymore."

The T. rex slowed down and closed in on them, sensing that his prey was now defeated.

"I don't think it matters anyway. We're trapped," replied Mike.

The T. rex eyed them closely. The beast leaned down and gave the duo a long hard sniff.

"I'm so sorry I got you involved with this," said Shannon. She reached over and squeezed Mike's arm tightly.

ROOOOOOOAAAAARRR!!

The sudden noise startled everyone, even the T. rex. The dinosaur stumbled around like a frightened animal. Leaves and branches scattered in every direction as the T. rex couldn't seem to get its footing.

Once it had gained some balance, the T. rex turned and quickly ran away.

Amazed, Mike watched the entire scene take place right in front of him. They could hear the T. rex whimpering its way back into the forest.

"Uh, what happened?" asked Mike.

Shannon looked at him equally puzzled. "I don't know." She moved towards Mike. "I was scared, so I reached over and grabbed your arm ..." She repeated the action, grabbing Mike's arm. "Like this."

"ROOOAARRR!!" A powerful growl erupted from Mike's Dino Jacket.

It was the same loud, rumbling roar that startled them and sent the T. rex running off like a scared rabbit.

"Your hoodie!" exclaimed Shannon.

"It roars!" finished Mike. "Sorry, I didn't know it could do that."

"Don't apologize!" Shannon smiled.

"For a second, I thought it was my video game," said Mike. "That thing goes off on its own sometimes."

Shannon hugged Mike more tightly than he had ever been hugged before. "You saved us!" she exclaimed.

Mike turned bright red. "I didn't mean to, but I think I did." Mike smiled. "I guess that's one of the amazing features my dad put in this jacket."

"Well, make sure you thank him for me!" said Shannon. "You know, that T. rex hasn't heard any other dinosaurs since it's been here. We're lucky your roar startled it. It's possible that it could have been attracted to the sound."

Mike brushed the leaves off his jacket. "So who was that boy back there?" he asked.

"Jurassic Jeff. Nothing but a troublemaker," Shannon explained.

"Jeff is from where I'm from," Shannon continued. "He thinks dinos should never have become extinct. He's trying to save them by introducing them back into different time periods. Unfortunately, he doesn't realize how much damage he's doing or how many people he's putting in danger. That's why I've come back here to stop him, and we were so close. We had caught the T. rex! Jeff must have known I was here and was following me."

"Let me get this straight," began Mike. "You came back here to capture a T. rex and take him back to his own time."

"Yes." Shannon nodded.

"Because he was stolen by a crazy boy who likes to call himself Jurassic Jeff?" Mike finished.

"Sounds strange, doesn't it?" she said.

Mike let out a deep breath. "If I hadn't just almost been eaten by a T. rex, I don't think I would have believed one word of your story." He was silent for a moment and then asked, "So what do we do now?"

"I can't ask for any more help than you've already given," said Shannon.

"Are you joking?" said Mike. "I always finish what I've started."

"Anyway," Mike continued, "now you have Jurassic Jeff running around and attempting to undo all your good work. I'm helping! I love dinosaurs too. It was fantastic to actually see one, but even I know it doesn't really belong here."

"That's so kind," said Shannon. "I knew when I saw you that I could trust you."

"Do you have more of those Trap-o-saur things?" asked Mike.

"Yes." Shannon nodded.

"Then what are we waiting for?" said Mike. "Let's go and get Sam!"

"Sam?" asked Shannon, confused.

Mike answered, "The T. rex."

"You've given the T. rex a name?" she asked again, still confused.

"We've been chased by him twice now. I feel like we know him," Mike explained.

Mike continued, "It feels strange to keep calling him the T. rex or the Dinosaur, so I've decided to give him a name ... you know, temporarily."

"Sam..." said Shannon. "I like it."

Chapter 8

BIG PROBLEMS

A short time later, the duo were approaching Shannon's campsite when Mike confessed. "I still can't believe that that boy calls himself Jurassic Jeff."

"There's nothing wrong with having a nickname," said Shannon.

"Oh yeah?" said Mike. "What should I call you ... Silly Shannon?"

"If you must make something up for me, you could be nicer," said Shannon. "I already have a nickname. My brother used to call me Triceratops Shannon."

Mike laughed. "Really? Triceratops Shannon?"

"There's a reason," she said, "but I don't know if I'm going to tell you now."

"Oh, come on!" encouraged Mike. "You have to now. You can't leave me with a name like Triceratops Shannon and not expect me to be curious."

As they crunched through the leaves, it was obvious that Shannon was a bit embarrassed.

"When I was little I would give myself funny hair styles," Shannon explained. "I would pull it into three ponytails so that it stuck up in the front and on the sides. It looked like I had three horns sticking out of my head that made me look like –"

Mike guessed and tried to finish her sentence. "A triceratops?"

"Yes, the three-horned dinosaur," confirmed Shannon.

"Hmm..." Mike rubbed his chin, puzzled. "I don't see the resemblance."

Shannon pulled her hair into spikes, and Mike laughed.

Mike didn't stop laughing until they reached the campsite. It was in tatters. Shannon's tent had been knocked over, and nearly everything inside it was broken.

The look on Shannon's face showed Mike that she was not surprised that the campsite had been destroyed.

"What happened?" asked Mike.

Shannon blurted out, "Jeff." She walked through the wreckage, picking up anything she could salvage. "He did this to make sure I wouldn't have any equipment to catch the T. rex."

"But all of your stuff," said Mike. "What are we going to do?"

Shannon looked at Mike. "When you've had a few run-ins with Jurassic Jeff, you learn to be prepared," she said.

Shannon picked up a small camping shovel and walked over to her broken tent. She flipped over the tent and started to dig underneath it.

"What are you doing?" asked Mike.

"Digging out the extra equipment I hid earlier," she said. "I knew Jeff might do something like this."

Mike smiled. "So you let Jeff destroy some things, but you have more hidden?"

"Yes," she answered. "Buried down here, underneath my tent."

"That's clever!" said Mike, complimenting her.

Shannon smiled. "Thanks. They don't call me Triceratops Shannon for nothing." She unearthed a box and pulled it up from the hole. "Triceratops are much cleverer than people think."

Shannon gathered all of the equipment from the box. She handed some to Mike.

"Now we need to find out where Sam is before people discover that there's a real dinosaur on the loose," she said.

Mike decided to be bolder with his questions. After all, they had been through quite a lot together by now. "So you come from a different time, do you?"

Shannon looked nervous for a moment. Then she said, "I really appreciate all the help you've given me. I've never met someone as nice and as helpful as you."

After a pause, Shannon said, "But I think the less you know about all of this stuff – who I am or where that dinosaur came from – the better."

"But..." Mike began.

Before he could say more, she continued. "I know it's not fair on you. If it was up to me, I would give you all the answers to your questions, but you're just going to have to trust me for now."

"Okay," said Mike. "If that's what you want."

A split second later, Shannon jumped towards Mike, tackling him into a giant bear hug.

Shannon realized she was squeezing Mike too hard and let him go. Her face turned red as they looked at each other in an awkward moment.

"So..." Mike said, breaking the silence, "are we going to look for Sam or what?"

Chapter 9
TROUBLE

Mike stood in the middle of an open area surrounded by trees. He was thinking about one of the last things Shannon had said to him: "The real question is, where's Jurassic Jeff?"

She had warned him that he could be anywhere and could surprise them at any time.

Mike reached over with his right hand and squeezed his left arm. The Dino Jacket let out a loud roar.

ROOOOAAAAR!

He was used to the sound now, but he was also making sure not to repeat it too many times. He squeezed the jacket again.

ROOOOAAAAR!

Mike looked around to make sure he couldn't see any red hair.

No. Good.

That meant Shannon had her hoodie on, hiding her hair. He knew she was hidden somewhere in the area.

If he couldn't see her, then Jurassic Jeff couldn't see her either.

"What are you doing out here?" came a voice from behind one of the trees.

"You should give up, Jeff," shouted Mike. "You may have ruined our plans to catch the T. rex the first time, but we finally caught it and now it's with Shannon."

"That's impossible!" Jeff screamed. He stepped out from behind the trees. "I've been tracking it. It was heading in this direction, and I also heard it roar."

"Oh, you mean *this* roar?" Mike said, squeezing the arm of his jacket again.

ROOOOAAAAR!

"How did you –?" said Jeff.

"From what I understand," said Mike, interrupting, "the sound should attract the T. rex here, making him think there are other dinosaurs."

As if on cue, the now-familiar sound of stomping and leaf crushing grew louder and louder behind them.

CRUNCH! SMASH! BOOM!

The T. rex Mike had nicknamed Sam burst through the thick foliage of the trees and into the open area. Mike could tell by the look on Jeff's face that he was surprised again.

As Sam stomped forwards, Mike did not want to miss his chance. He threw down a trap. It quickly unfolded into a blue see-through cube. Before Sam realized what was happening, the dinosaur was trapped inside.

"HEY!" shouted Jeff. "That's my dinosaur!"

Jeff started running towards Mike with what Mike could only assume was the same laser-knife he had used to cut Sam free from the last trap.

"I thought you said that Shannon had already trapped him!" screamed Jeff.

"We tricked you!" said Shannon.

She came running out of the trees, pulling off her hoodie to reveal her red hair so that Jeff could be sure that it was her. As she got closer, she threw down another trap. This one landed directly in Jeff's path.

The big blue cube erected itself just as Jeff stepped into it. Jurassic Jeff was now as motionless as the T. rex.

"Wow! I can't believe that worked," said Shannon, giving a deep sigh of relief. "I contacted my team, and they should be arriving at my campsite any minute now."

"What are we waiting for?" said Mike. "Let's get going!"

Shannon gave Mike one last hug and said, "Thanks for everything."

Mike looked over at Jeff and realized that he had activated the laser cutter he was holding in his hand. He was cutting his way out of the cube.

"RUN!" shouted Mike as he pushed Shannon towards the T. rex.

Shannon put her hands on the blue cube and pushed it towards the forest.

Mike had never seen anything like it. A large blue-edged cube with a life-size T. rex inside of it rolled through the forest, hovering just above the ground.

As Shannon effortlessly pushed the cube along, Mike followed right behind her. He was sure that Jurassic Jeff was not far behind him.

"Get to the campsite!" said Mike.

"What about you?" asked Shannon.

"Don't worry about me," replied Mike. "You get out of here and get Sam back where he belongs. I'll distract Jeff."

Shannon continued to roll the giant caged T. rex through the forest. Mike heard her say, "Thank you..." But he couldn't hear the rest of her sentence as she disappeared into the forest.

Without wasting any more time, Mike pulled a large pile of leaves over him. He hid down among the leaves.

All was quiet for a few seconds until he heard the trampling of sticks and leaves. It was Jeff, hot on their trail.

Mike waited until Jeff was almost on top of him, and then he surprised him. Mike burst out of the leaves, pulling his hoodie up over his head.

Beep! Beep! The T. rex eyes on Mike's hoodie activated. The blinding light shined right in Jeff's face.

"Ahhhhh!! My eyes!" screamed Jeff. "I can't see!" He rubbed his eyes, trying to regain his vision.

Mike used the opportunity to run and catch up with Shannon.

"You may have blinded me with those bright lights for a few seconds, but I can still hear you!" shouted Jeff.

He's right! thought Mike. *If he can hear my footsteps and I try to follow Shannon, he'll catch us and get the T. rex back again.*

Jeff was bleary-eyed but could finally see again. "My vision is back!" he exclaimed. "Now I'll find you –"

But he didn't see anyone as he looked around. "Where are you?" Jeff shouted.

Jeff looked behind one tree and then another. He looked behind all the trees in the area but couldn't see anyone.

"You're just wasting time. I'll find you..." He stopped. "Oh no. That's what you wanted. You wanted me to follow you so I wouldn't follow her. You tricked me into looking for you to give Shannon extra time to snatch the T. rex."

Jeff realized that the minutes he had spent looking for Mike had given Shannon enough time to get away.

"Arghh!" shouted Jeff, shaking his hand in the air. "You're nothing but trouble!"

Jeff stomped off. "You'd better hope we never meet again!" he mumbled and grumbled his way through the forest.

Mike could hear less and less of Jeff's complaints the further away he got. The reason Jeff couldn't find him hiding behind any of the trees was because he wasn't behind a tree...

He was *up* a tree!

Mike had hardly moved away from the pile of leaves he had been hiding in.

He realized Jeff was right.

He had temporarily blinded Jeff, but Mike could still hear what direction he was going in. Mike used his retractable dinosaur claws and climbed instead.

Luckily for him, Jeff never thought to look up.

Chapter 10

DINO EGGS!

Mike made his way to Shannon's campsite. There was no sign of her ever having been there except for the bit they had dug up to find her hidden equipment. Even the soil had been smoothed over.

Shannon's departure must have gone to plan, and she was able to get where she needed to be with Sam the T. rex.

Mike thought about the day's adventure as he made his way back through the forest to the dig site where his father was working. He probably didn't have to worry about Jurassic Jeff anymore either. As Shannon and Sam the T. rex had both gone, Jeff had probably disappeared too.

He wasn't going to miss Jeff, or the big scary dinosaur ... but as for his other friend, Triceratops Shannon, he really would miss her.

As he approached the dig site, he noticed that it was getting dark. The science teams were packing up their equipment for the night.

Mike looked over at the large tree on the other side of the dig site. That was the tree he decided to climb when he first spotted the mysterious stranger, Shannon. Even though he knew her now, he still thought of her as a mysterious stranger because he didn't know much about her or where she was from.

Mike smiled because that was the tree that had changed his life. That's where he'd first spotted Sam the T. rex.

Mike turned around to look at the forest. He wasn't standing far from the spot where he had first seen the tail of that giant lizard. Just a few metres away behind those trees was where the T. rex, from a time long past, had been stomping around just a few short hours ago.

He walked over to the edge of the dig site and saw all the flags and posts marking where bones were buried. He could see people working to dig up the bones of a dinosaur similar to the one he had seen walking around just a moment ago. It was hard to believe that millions of years later this is how dinos would end up.

He looked down and saw a large grassy area. As his eyes swept the spot, something white caught his attention. At first he thought that they were just rocks piled in the grass. Then he noticed that the way they were clumped together looked odd.

Mike decided to take a closer look. The rocks were strange. They almost looked more like giant eggs than they did rocks. He was about to reach down and pick one up when he suddenly heard a familiar voice.

"Mike?" Mike turned to see his dad coming towards him. He was walking along the edge of the dig site. Mike was easy to spot in the middle of the open area of grass between the edge of the dig site and the forest.

"I've been looking for you everywhere, Mike. The barbecue is about to start. You must be hungry."

"Yes, I am!" replied Mike, realizing that he hadn't eaten all day.

"Hey, what's that?" his dad asked as he got closer.

Mike looked down at the odd-shaped rocks at his feet.

"I'm not sure," said Mike, "but I think they're eggs."

Mike could see his dad's eyes grow to almost twice their normal size.

"Dad? What's the matter?" said Mike.

"Mike!" exclaimed his dad. "You have just discovered some dinosaur eggs!"

"Really?!" cried Mike.

His dad took a closer look. "These are so well preserved too! I've never seen anything like this before!"

He shouted down to the team packing up equipment on the dig site. "We've got something over here! Bring up some lights and equipment as fast as you can!"

Dad turned to Mike and held him excitedly by the shoulders. "This is incredible! The first day I've ever brought you on a dinosaur dig, and you've made one of the biggest finds ever!"

Just then, beeping sounds started coming from Mike's pocket.

Dad laughed and patted Mike on the back. "Don't you ever turn that video game off?" He turned to give his team instructions on how to proceed. Then he ended by saying to Mike, "Museums all over the world are going to go crazy!"

Mike smiled. After the day he'd had he didn't think it could get any better, and now this?

It was incredible! The video game in his pocket beeped loudly again.

Thinking that he had forgotten to turn it off, Mike pulled it out of his pocket.

The screen read, "Hello, Mike!"

That was strange. He pressed the buttons, and the message scrolled down. It read: "Hope you don't mind, but I found your game frequency. I thought I would send you a message letting you know how much I appreciate your help! Also how unfair it was that you had to deal with Jurassic Jeff by yourself, and that you found out my nickname was Triceratops (LOL). Anyway, I have decided that you need a nickname too! Thanks again for all your help ... DINO-MIKE!"

Mike scrolled down to the bottom of the message.

"P.S.: Sam the T. rex got home safely. FYI: Sam is actually Samantha! Isn't that funny!"

Mike laughed to himself. Then, something suddenly occurred to him.

Mike's face went blank as he watched his dad and his team lift the eggs and place them into a padded box.

He thought, *Sam is actually ... a GIRL!!*

Sam the T. rex wasn't coming to the dig site to look for food. Samantha the T. rex was coming to the dig site to look after her eggs!

As the box was sealed shut, Mike whispered, "Uh-oh."

Time for another adventure! thought Dino-Mike.

GLOSSARY

extinct something that no longer exists;
an animal or bird is extinct when there are
no more examples of it alive

fossil remains or traces of an animal or
plant from millions of years ago, preserved
in rock

Jurassic Period period of time about 200
to 144 million years ago

palaeontologist scientist who studies
extinct animals and plants and their fossils

triceratops large, plant-eating dinosaur
with three horns and a fan-shaped collar
of bone

tyrannosaurus large, meat-eating dinosaur
that walked on its hind legs, also known as
a T. rex

DINO FACTS!

Did you know that the scientific name tyrannosaurus rex means "Tyrant Lizard King"? Weighing 4 to 6 metric tons (that's more than 4,000 kilograms), this dino really was reptile royalty.

The T. rex was the star of the film *Jurassic Park*, but these dinos didn't actually live during the Jurassic Period. They lived between 65 to 85 million years ago during a time known as the Cretaceous period.

At 12 metres long and 6 metres tall, the T. rex was one of the largest meat-eating dinos ever.

Scientists believe T. rex could chase its prey at more than 65 kilometres an hour.

The T. rex's arms were surprisingly small. At only 90 centimetres long, they were too short to catch prey. Instead of grabbing prey with its tiny arms, T. rex grabbed food with its teeth. Each T. rex tooth measured more than 20 centimetres long!

T. rex used its giant teeth to satisfy a giant appetite. With one bite, scientists believe the T. rex could gobble up about 200 kilograms of meat.

All of the T. rex fossils ever discovered have been found in North America. In 1990, one of the best-known and most complete skeletons was discovered in the state of South Dakota, USA, by fossil hunter Sue Hendrickson. The fossil, known simply as "Sue," is now on display at the Field Museum in Chicago, USA.

ABOUT THE AUTHOR

New York-born author and artist Franco Aureliani has been drawing comics since he could hold a crayon. Currently residing in upstate New York, USA, with his wife, Ivette, and son, Nicolas, he spends most of his days in his Batcave-like studio where he works on comic projects. In 1995, Franco founded Blindwolf Studios, an independent art studio where he and fellow creators can create children's comics. Franco is the creator, artist and author of Weirdsville, L'il Creeps and Eagle All Star, as well as the co-creator and author of Patrick the Wolf Boy.

Franco recently finished work on Superman Family Adventures and is now co-writing the series The Green Team: Teen Trillionaires and Tiny Titans by DC Comics. When he's not writing and drawing, Franco teaches secondary school art.